The Littlest Dinosaur at the Big Carnival

By Charyl Friedman

Illustrated by
Elizabeth DiGregorio and Hal Toledo

In memory of Hal Toledo,
my mentor, muse, and art director.
—Elizabeth

Copyright © 1993 Kidsbooks, Inc.
3535 West Peterson Avenue
Chicago, IL 60659

Manufactured in the United States of America

"The carnival is coming to town! The carnival is coming to town!" shouted Albert, the littlest dinosaur.

"Are you sure?" asked his best friend Billie.

"It says so right here on this poster," said Albert. "Big Carnival! Best Rides! Best Games! Best Food!"

"And it starts in just two days," said Billie as the two ran off to spread the word.

By the end of the day, everyone at school knew about the big carnival and they were all excited.

"I'm going to ride the Roller Roaster," said Albert.

"I'm going to eat the biggest candy apple," said Billie.

"I'm going to win the best prize at the Boulderball Booth," said Rocco.

"I'm going to go into the Haunted House," said Freddy. "I think."

That night Albert went home and emptied out his cave bank. He had saved all his birthday money for a good reason. Admission to the big carnival was the best reason he could think of.

When he was through, Albert climbed into bed, closed his eyes, and wished for morning to come so it would be one day closer to the big carnival.

As Albert and Billie walked to school the next day they saw the carnival trucks coming into town.

"Here it comes," shouted Albert. "There's the Roller Roaster and the Dino Wheel and the Happy-Go-Round."

"There's the cotton candy booth and the ice treat corner and the peanut stand," said Billie. She was going to eat something from all of them.

"And tomorrow the carnival begins and we'll be there," said Albert as the two skipped the rest of the way to school.

It was finally here. The day the big carnival began. Albert and Billie were up bright and early so they could be the first ones there when the carnival opened.

"What should we do first?" asked Albert when they were let in.
"There's the Happy-Go-Round. Let's go on that first," said Billie.

After the Happy-Go-Round, the two friends stopped for ice-treat cones.

"Yummy!" said Billie as she took a big bite of her cone. "I could easily eat another one of these! What flavor did you get, Albert?"

"It's called Dino's Delight," Albert said as he ate a little faster.

The two finished their ice treats in no time and ran off to find more fun.

Next, the two friends passed the Haunted House.

"Do you want to go in?" asked Albert.

"Okay," said Billie. But then suddenly, they saw Freddy come running out of the Haunted House screaming as loud as can be. He was being chased by a ghost!

"Maybe next year," said Albert as he and Billie headed off in another direction—fast!

"Look, there's the Roller Roaster," said Albert. "That's the ride I want to go on most!"
Billie and Albert waited on a long line until finally they were next.
"I'm sorry, but you can't go on this ride," the ticket seller said to Albert.
"What do you mean?" asked Albert. "This is the ride
I've been waiting for."
"See that sign over there? You have to be at least that tall to go on this
ride, and you don't measure up. But your friend can ride,"
he answered.

Must Be This Tall

**ROLLER
ROASTER
RIDE**

Must Be This Tall

"But, but my friend and I are the same age, and, and I'm not afraid," said Albert. "I'm just short!"

"Sorry, but those are the rules," said the man. "Come back next year when you've grown some."

"Who wants to go on that dumb ride anyway," said Billie as they walked away. "We'll have much more fun on the Dino Wheel."

But when the two friends got to the Dino Wheel, they saw the same sign.

"I'm not tall enough for this ride either," moaned Albert. "When will I ever grow?"

"There are lots of other rides here," said Billie. "We'll go on those," she added trying to cheer him up.

"Those rides are for babies!" said Albert. "You go on the Dino Wheel. I just want to be alone for awhile," he said as he walked away.

Albert was angry. Very angry. Why did the fact that he was so little always get in the way? Just once he wanted to feel like a big dinosaur.

After a while Albert got tired of wandering around. As he passed the Friendly Flyers ride he decided to go on.

Albert waited on line and was about to step into his flyer when he heard someone crying behind him.

"What's wrong?" Albert asked as he turned toward the young dinosaur.

"I thought I was big enough to go on this by myself, but now that I'm here, I'm scared," he answered.

"This is a fun ride," said Albert. "You'll see. You can ride with me."

"What's your name?" Albert asked when the ride was over.

"My friends call me J.J.," he answered.

"Well J.J.," said Albert. "That wasn't too bad, was it?"

"It was great!" said J.J. "But that's because I went with a big dinosaur like you."

Albert broke into a big grin. "I'll be happy to go on any other rides with you, but first I have to find my friend Billie," he said.

"I'm going to get some cotton candy," said J.J. "I'll wait for you there."

"Big dinosaur!" thought a beaming Albert as he looked for Billie. "He called me a big dinosaur. I guess you don't have to be tall after all."

Suddenly Albert spotted her. "Billie," he called as he ran up to his friend. "I'm sorry I walked away. I was angry, but it wasn't your fault."

"It's okay," said Billie. "Are you feeling better now?"

"You bet I am," said Albert. "Come on, and I'll introduce you to the reason why."